Martha's New School

Danielle Steel
Martha's New School

Illustrated by Jacqueline Rogers

Delacorte Press

Published by
Delacorte Press
Bantam Doubleday Dell Publishing Group, Inc.
666 Fifth Avenue
New York, New York 10103

Library of Congress Cataloging in Publication Data

Steel, Danielle.
  Martha's new school / by Danielle Steel; illustrated by
Jacqueline Rogers.
    p. cm.
  Summary: When six-year-old Martha moves with her mother
and new stepfather to Sausalito, she dreads going to a new school,
but finds it a very pleasant experience after all.
  ISBN 0-385-29800-5
  [1. Schools—Fiction.] I. Rogers, Jacqueline, ill. II. Title.
PZ7.S8143Mar 1989
[E]—dc19   88-36605
                                     CIP
                                     AC

design by Judith Neuman-Cantor

Manufactured in the United States of America

November 1989

10 9 8 7 6 5 4 3 2

To Victoria, precious love, special baby, special big girl now!

With all my love,
Mommy

This is Martha. She is six years old,
and she lives in San Francisco.

She has lived here all her life, in the
same house.

She has gone to the same school
for kindergarten and first grade,
and she loves it.

Martha's Mommy and Daddy have been divorced for a long time. That means that they aren't married anymore, but they're still friends. Last year, Martha's Mommy married a man named John. Martha loves him a lot.

Martha lives with her Mommy and John in the house she's lived in ever since she was a baby.

Martha loves her Daddy too. She sees him every week on Wednesday nights, and on some weekends. They spend holidays like Christmas together, and they go away for a month together every summer.

But now, Martha's Mommy and John want to move to a new house. It is across the Golden Gate Bridge in a little town called Sausalito. It's only twenty minutes away from Martha's old house in San Francisco, but it looks very different. It has a wonderful view of the bay. And the boats. On a clear day, Martha can see both bridges in San Francisco: the Golden Gate and the Bay Bridge.

Martha saw the new house when John and her Mommy bought it, and she really liked it. It was a beautiful white house with a garden full of flowers. And she was going to have a big pink bedroom full of white furniture that her Mommy and John had painted just for her.

What she didn't like was that now she
would have to go to a new school in
Sausalito. She wanted to keep going to
her old school. But her Mommy said it
was too far away. It would be too hard
for Martha to go back and forth to San
Francisco every day. So now she'll be
going to a new school in September.

Martha was very sad about leaving her
friends at her old school. Her Mommy
promised that she would still see her
old friends.

They would even come to see her in Sausalito. And Martha's Mommy told her that soon she would have a lot of new friends. But it wasn't just leaving her old friends that worried Martha. There were lots of other things to worry about too. Martha worried about all of them: she worried about whether the teacher would be mean or nice, or if there would be too much homework, or what would happen if she didn't make any friends at all. What if no one even spoke to her once she got there? What if the lunches were terrible? Or, worse yet, what if she couldn't find the bathroom? There were a thousand things to worry about, and as summer passed, Martha got more and more worried about her new school.

By the time the first day of school rolled around, Martha was so worried and so scared, she could hardly keep from crying as her Mommy drove her to school on the first morning. All she could think of was how scared she was. She sat in the front seat of the car. The palms of her hands felt wet. Her stomach felt sick. She couldn't think of anything except how terrible and how scary it was to be at her new school, instead of her old one.

Martha's Mommy walked her into the school. Then a teacher walked Martha into the classroom. With a last wave and a smile, her Mommy was gone. Martha was alone with a school full of strangers.

As Martha walked into the room, she looked around. She saw a familiar face in the back corner. It was Sally, whose Daddy was a friend of John's. They had all gone sailing together once during the summer. Martha remembered liking her, and she was excited there was someone she knew. Sally waved.

When Martha looked around again,
she saw a little boy she had seen before
at the doctor's office. And all of a
sudden she remembered that one of her
friends from her old school went to this
school now, too. At least, Martha thought
with a sigh, there were a few people
she knew here.

The teacher seemed very nice, too.
Her name was Mrs. Thomas, and she
had a nice smile and Martha liked her.
She welcomed Martha to the class. She
showed her where everything was, even
the bathroom.

Then she introduced Martha and two
other new girls and a new boy to everyone
in the class.

At recess, she came over and asked Martha if she would like some juice and cookies. Martha decided that her new teacher wasn't as pretty as her old teacher. Still, she was so nice that Martha wondered if eventually she would like her better. She had a nice smile, and Martha liked the way Mrs. Thomas put her arm around her shoulders.

At lunchtime, Sally came over and asked Martha to have lunch with her. Before Martha had even finished her sandwich, Sally had introduced her to almost everyone in their class. Soon they were all talking and making lots of noise. They promised to have their Mommies call Martha's Mommy, so they could invite Martha to play.

It was a good first day of school for Martha. She liked her teacher, she liked her new friends, she liked her new school and the things they did. Everyone in her class had talked to her, and she really liked them. The best thing was that it wasn't a scary place at all. The people weren't scary either. It was a nice school, and by the time her Mommy came to pick her up she knew that she was really going to like it.

"How was school?" Her Mommy looked
at her with a serious face.

"It was nice." Martha smiled at her.

"Did you make any new friends?"

Martha nodded, smiling at her Mommy.
"Yes, I did." She told her about Sally
and all the others, and how nice the
school was. "Can I have them over
sometime, Mommy?"

"Sure." Her Mommy promised to have
someone over to play that weekend.

That night, just before Martha went to sleep, Sally called. And Martha ran into her Mommy's bedroom to talk to her on the phone.

"Hi, Martha. I just called to say good night and tell you I'll see you at school tomorrow."

"That was really nice of you." The two girls promised to have lunch together the next day.

When Martha climbed back into bed, and her Mommy tucked her in, she yawned. She was thinking of Sally, and school, and all her new friends. She smiled to herself, remembering how scared she had been about her new school only that morning. But none of her terrible fears had come true. Her teacher wasn't scary and mean. Instead she was gentle and nice. The children had been welcoming and warm, and none of the things Martha had worried about had happened. It was a good lesson for Martha to learn that her new school was an interesting, happy place, full of new and exciting people. They were just waiting to be Martha's friends, and she really liked them. Maybe not as much as her old friends just yet, but she knew that eventually she would love them just as much as she loved her old friends.

In time, she knew that her new school would be a wonderful place to go, and all her friends there would become very special to her.